JAN 2 1

Hispanic
IN AMERICA

Jim Gallagher

San Diego, CA

About the Author

Jim Gallagher is the author of more than twenty books for young adults. The titles, written for various publishers, include *The Johnstown Flood*, *Causes of the Iraq War*, *Illegal Immigration*, and *Refugees and Asylum*. He lives in central New Jersey with his wife, LaNelle, and their three children.

© 2021 ReferencePoint Press, Inc.
Printed in the United States

For more information, contact:
ReferencePoint Press, Inc.
PO Box 27779
San Diego, CA 92198
www.ReferencePointPress.com

LIBRARY OF CONGRESS CATALOGING-IN-PUBLICATION DATA

Names: Gallagher, Jim, 1969- author.
Title: Hispanic in America / by Jim Gallagher.
Description: San Diego, CA : ReferencePoint Press, Inc., [2021] | Series: Bias in America | Includes bibliographical references and index.
Identifiers: LCCN 2020017066 (print) | LCCN 2020017067 (ebook) | ISBN 9781682828939 (library binding) | ISBN 9781682828946 (ebook)
Subjects: LCSH: Hispanic Americans--Ethnic identity--Juvenile literature. | Hispanic Americans--Social conditions--Juvenile literature. | Hispanic Americans--Race identity--Juvenile literature. | Racism--United States--History--Juvenile literature. | United States--Race relations--History--Juvenile literature. | United States--Ethnic relations--Juvenile literature.
Classification: LCC E184.S75 G35 2021 (print) | LCC E184.S75 (ebook) | DDC 305.868/073--dc23
LC record available at https://lccn.loc.gov/2020017066
LC ebook record available at https://lccn.loc.gov/2020017067

CONTENTS

Murders in El Paso

On the morning of Saturday, August 3, 2019, about one thousand people were browsing the aisles of the Walmart Supercenter on Gateway Boulevard in El Paso, Texas. The start of school was just a few weeks away, so the shoppers were taking advantage of sales on pencils, notebooks, backpacks, and other school supplies. Many were residents of El Paso, a city of nearly seven hundred thousand located along the Rio Grande, the river that marks the border between Texas and Mexico. Hundreds of others had come from Ciudad Juárez, the Mexican city right across the river, which has a population of nearly 1.4 million. It is common for residents of the two cities to cross the border to take advantage of sales in local stores, visit family members, or enjoy cultural events.

One person at the Walmart that morning had come from much farther away. Twenty-one-year-old Patrick Crusius had driven more than ten hours from his home in a Dallas suburb. Crusius was not interested in school supplies. A white nationalist, he believed Hispanics and other people of color were genetically inferior to whites. Believing that the "pure" culture of America was being overwhelmed by a flood of immigrants, Crusius had come to El Paso to strike back against what he called the "Hispanic invasion of Texas."[1]

At around 10:39 a.m., Crusius opened fire in the Walmart parking lot with an AK-47-style semiautomatic rifle. Targeting his fire at Hispanic-looking persons, he worked his way into the crowded store. Panicked shoppers dove for cover, hiding behind shelves or running for the exits. In less than ten minutes, Crusius shot and killed twenty-two people. Among the victims were Javier Amir Rodriguez, an American teen who loved soccer and was preparing to start his sophomore year of high school in El Paso; Juan de Dios Velázquez, a seventy-seven-year-old Mexican retiree who was shot trying to protect his wife; and Jordan and Andre Anchondo, a young married couple from El Paso who had left their infant son and six-year-old daughter at home. Twenty-seven others were wounded before Crusius surrendered to police outside the store. It was the deadliest attack targeting Hispanics in recent US history, and it was motivated by bigotry and hate.

A memorial wall honors the victims of the August 2019 shooting rampage at a Walmart in El Paso, Texas. The gunman freely admitted to police that his goal was to kill Hispanics.

Rising Hate Toward Hispanics

Shortly before his attack, Crusius had posted a four-page manifesto to an online message board. It expressed his belief in the "Great Replacement," a white supremacist theory that claims a group of elites is secretly trying to destroy white populations in Europe and the United States by replacing them with nonwhite immigrants and refugees. Crusius expressed disgust with "race-mixing" and Hispanic immigration, and he criticized the economic and environmental policies of Democrats, Republicans, and corporate America. "Hispanics will take control of the local and state government of my beloved Texas, changing policy to better suit their needs," he wrote. "They will turn Texas into an instrument of a political coup which will hasten the destruction of our country."[2] After his attack, Crusius freely admitted to police that his goal was to kill Hispanics.

Some people contend that white supremacist beliefs are confined to the fringes of American society. Others, however, believe that in recent years an increase in right-wing, anti-immigrant political rhetoric has emboldened white nationalists like Crusius to attack Hispanics. "There's a direct correlation between the hate speech and fear-mongering coming from President Trump and the right wing of the Republican Party with the increase in attacks against Latinos,"[3] said Domingo Garcia, president of the League of United Latin American Citizens.

> "There's a direct correlation between . . . hate speech and fear-mongering [and] the increase in attacks against Latinos."[3]
>
> —Domingo Garcia, president of the League of United Latin American Citizens

Statistics gathered by federal law enforcement agencies show that Hispanics are among the groups most commonly attacked in America today. In November 2019, the FBI reported that the number of hate crimes targeting Hispanics had reached a sixteen-year high during the previous year. Hate crimes involve assaults, murders, and other criminal offenses that are primarily motivated by the victim's race, religion, ethnicity, sexual orientation, or other identifier. The FBI reported that hate crimes against Hispanics have been rising since 2015.

Driven by Nativism

Unfortunately, violent attacks on Hispanic Americans are nothing new. The United States has a long history of discrimination against Hispanics. Bias toward Hispanics is often driven by xenophobia, a fear or hatred of people or cultures that are different from one's own. In the United States, this concern about foreigners and immigrants is often identified with the term *nativism*.

Nativism originated in nineteenth-century America. Its adherents, known as nativists, believe that American culture should be homogeneous—that is, that only those who share their social customs, language, beliefs, and historical experiences can be considered "true" Americans. Anyone different is an "outsider" to be feared and shunned. Nativists demand that those who wish to live in the United States assimilate completely, exchanging their native languages for English and their traditional customs and beliefs for what nativists believe are the white, English-speaking, Protestant Christian ethics and morals promoted by the nation's founders. Those who do not, or cannot, assimilate for racial, ethnic, or religious reasons are often attacked as being un-American.

"To the racist nativist, Latino native-born US citizens living in the United States are perceived as outsiders because of their Spanish surnames, non-Anglo culture, and non-Anglo physical appearance," explains historian Camilo M. Ortiz. "They are thus unlike European immigrants who were considered foreigners by eighteenth and nineteenth century nativists, but were nevertheless, able successfully to assimilate into the dominant Anglo culture because they were not immigrants of color. Seen in this light, anti-Latino violence is particularly intractable because Latinos find themselves at the center of both nativism and racism."[4]

CHAPTER ONE

A History of Second-Class Citizenship

Spanish-speaking people lived in North America more than one hundred years before the first permanent British settlements were established during the seventeenth century. Spain's New World colonies in the American West and Southwest were lightly populated, however, unlike the thirteen American colonies along the Eastern Seaboard that declared independence in 1776. At that time, the United States was predominantly made up of English-speaking settlers of white European descent; they are often called Anglo-Americans, or Anglos, to differentiate them from the Spanish-speaking, or Hispanic, population of North America.

As the US population grew during the nineteenth century, Anglo-Americans began to expand their settlements westward into lands where Hispanics and Native Americans lived. The United States gained some land through negotiations, such as the Louisiana Purchase from France (1803) or the acquisition of Florida from Spain (1819). By the 1840s, however, many Americans embraced the nativist idea that their white Protestant Anglo-American culture was superior to all others and that it was the "manifest destiny" of the United States to stretch from the Atlantic to the Pacific Oceans—by conquest, if necessary.

In 1845, the United States annexed the Republic of Texas, which had won independence from Mexico nine years earlier. The Mexican government still claimed Texas, however, so when US troops arrived in the region, war broke out. The Mexican–American War (1846–1848) ended with the victorious Americans forcing Mexico to cede more than one-third of its territory to the United States. Under the terms of the Treaty of Guadalupe Hidalgo, the United States gained the land known as Alta (Upper) California, as well as parts of New Mexico, Arizona, Nevada, Utah, and Colorado. The land transfer brought 75,000 to 100,000 Mexicans under the jurisdiction of the United States, along with about 150,000 Native Americans.

The treaty allowed the Mexicans in the now American territories to decide whether they wanted to remain in their homes in the United States or relocate to Mexico. It guaranteed that those who stayed would eventually become US

US and Mexican forces meet in battle during the Mexican-American War. With the US victory came new territory and a chance for thousands of Mexicans to become US citizens.

citizens and could keep land they had owned before the war. The treaty promised that these Hispanics would be "maintained and protected in the free enjoyment of their liberty and property, and secured in the free exercise of their religion without restriction."[5]

When the treaty was signed in 1848, Hispanics outnumbered Anglos in Alta California; however, the discovery of gold at Sutter's Mill (near modern-day Sacramento) later that year led to a massive influx of eastern Americans, as well as foreign immigrants from China, South America, and other countries. Over the next two years, the population of California grew from a few thousand to more than one hundred thousand, making it eligible for statehood. Many of the newcomers were Anglos, but landowning *Californios* (as the Mexican Americans who lived in the territory were known) still had political power. Eight *Californios* were among the forty-eight delegates elected to the 1849 convention that drafted the first state constitution. They pushed to include provisions protecting the rights of *Californios*, such as a requirement that all laws be published in both Spanish and English.

Discrimination Through Law

But promises of equality were soon forgotten as more settlers moved west. Anglos used the legal system, as well as racist policies, to control the government and marginalize Hispanics and other minorities. Compounding the problem, many Hispanics were confused by the American justice system or unable to communicate properly with English-speaking officials. As a result, Mexican Americans were routinely cheated out of property in California and elsewhere in the Southwest.

Prior to 1846, more than eight hundred of the wealthiest *Californios* lived on enormous tracts of land called ranchos, which had been granted to them by the Mexican government. Each of these *ranchos* covered about 14 square miles (36 sq. km) and was used for grazing sheep or cattle. Under Mexican rule, the *Californios* had paid taxes based on their *rancho*'s annual production, not its size. The new state legislature, however, changed this system by

Discrimination Against Tejanos

In 1835, rebels in Texas began fighting for independence from Mexico. Most were Anglo-Americans, known as Texians, who had relatively recently settled in Texas. But there also were some Hispanic residents, or Tejanos. Several Tejanos signed the Texas Declaration of Independence on March 2, 1836. Others died with the Texian garrison at the Alamo on March 6 or fought with the Texians at the Battle of San Jacinto six weeks later—a victory that ensured Texas's independence as the Republic of Texas.

At first, Tejanos were represented in the new republic's government. Juan Seguín, a war hero, was among several Tejanos elected to the Texas legislature. The legislature passed a measure requiring laws in Texas to be printed in both Spanish and English. Tejanos also controlled most of the seats on the city council that governed San Antonio, Texas's largest city. But continued immigration of Anglo-Americans, as well as fears that Tejanos would not be loyal to the new republic in ongoing conflict with Mexico, resulted in an erosion of their rights. As Anglos gained control, they created laws making it hard for Tejanos to vote or to keep their land. "They became a suspect class," explains Raúl Ramos, a history professor at the University of Houston. "The idea was that they couldn't be fully Texan or fully American."

Discouraged by oppression, in 1842 Seguín moved back to Mexico. There, due to his skill as a soldier, he was conscripted into the Mexican Army. Seguín reluctantly fought against US forces when the Mexican-American War began in 1846.

Quoted in Becky Little, "Why Mexican Americans Say 'the Border Crossed Us,'" History Channel website, October 17, 2018. www.history.com.

imposing a property tax. Most *Californios* could not afford to pay the new tax on their *rancho* and had to sell off some of their lands.

Another problem was that when Anglo miners and homesteaders arrived in the state, they often squatted on *ranchos* legally owned by Mexican Americans. Rather than evicting these illegal settlers, the federal government passed a law in 1851 that required *Californios* to prove their land grants were valid. The process was expensive and could take many years to complete. *Californios* often had to borrow money at high interest rates or sell off parts of their *ranchos* just to prove their homes were rightfully theirs.

Although Hispanics in California were American citizens, their rights were gradually restricted by laws and court decisions during the 1850s. For example, *Californios* had to pay the Foreign Miners' Tax of 1850, a monthly fee of $20 (about $650 in today's dollars) imposed on immigrants but not on Anglo-Americans. In 1854 the California Supreme Court ruled in *People v. Hall* that Chinese immigrants could not testify in court against whites; by 1857 this ruling had been extended to include Hispanic testimony as well. An 1855 anti-vagrancy law specifically targeted Mexican Americans, making it illegal for them to gather in large groups; those found in violation of the law could be sentenced to forced labor and have their lands seized by the state. And an 1857 law negated the state constitutional requirement that state and local laws had to be rendered in both Spanish and English.

"Not surprisingly, the laws were enforced unequally throughout much of the nineteenth century."[6]

—Linda Heidenreich, historian

Other laws sought to curtail Hispanic cultural and religious practices, writes historian Linda Heidenreich:

> The 1850s also saw the first wide-scale passage and enforcement of Blue Laws, based on white Protestant religion and culture. The state enacted a law against bull, bear, and cock fights, as well as circuses and other "noisy amusements." . . . Law enforcement authorities and the courts—both predominantly Anglo and Protestant—decided when to make arrests and how much to fine perpetrators on a case-by-case basis. Not surprisingly, the laws were enforced unequally throughout much of the nineteenth century.[6]

By 1870, continued settlement by Anglos meant that Hispanics made up just 4 percent of California's population. Due to their low numbers, they rarely had political representation. Most Hispanics were poor tenant farmers, working on land owned by Anglos. In California and other western states and territories, Anglos and Hispanics usually lived separately, with Mexican American neighborhoods, or barrios, having their own schools, stores, churches, and places of entertainment.

Vigilante Justice in the Southwest

Anglos also used extralegal means to oppress the Hispanic population. From the 1840s to the 1930s, thousands of Hispanics were victims of lynching and other mob violence. "The scale of mob violence against Mexicans is staggering," note history professors William D. Carrigan and Clive Webb, "far exceeding the violence exacted on any other immigrant group and comparable, at least on a per-capita basis, to the mob violence suffered by African Americans."[7]

Lynching was intended to reinforce white supremacy in a given region. To maintain control of the gold mining industry, Anglo miners murdered at least 163 Hispanics in California from 1848 to 1860. Carrigan and Webb report that Texas had the most lynching incidents, but these horrible murders occurred in every southwestern state.

Hispanic Americans were lynched for a variety of reasons. Some were accused of murder, rape, cattle rustling, theft, or cheating at cards. Others were killed because they had jobs or land that Anglos wanted or simply because they were different. "The justification for lynching Latinas/os tended to be very similar to the motives behind lynching African Americans, such as posing a threat to white women," writes historian José Luis Morín. "Latina/o lynchings, however, also were occasioned

> "The scale of mob violence against Mexicans is staggering, far exceeding the violence exacted on any other immigrant group and comparable, at least on a per-capita basis, to the mob violence suffered by African Americans."[7]
>
> —William D. Carrigan and Clive Webb, history professors

by a person speaking Spanish or exhibiting another public display of distinct Latina/o cultural identity,"[8] he adds.

Occasionally, lynchings were conducted publicly to remind Hispanics of their subservient relationship to whites. In 1874, a mob in Brownsville, Texas, hanged two Hispanic men for theft and left their bodies on display in the street for several days. Most of the time, however, lynchings were quieter affairs. In the sparsely populated Southwest, it might be days or weeks before the bodies of victims were discovered.

The federal government rarely investigated lynchings during the nineteenth and twentieth centuries, because individual states have jurisdiction in murder cases. But because lynchings often had the unspoken support of local communities, Anglo authorities were able to forestall most investigations. "The lynching of Mexicans . . . was based on the belief in the Anglo-American community that it was a 'civic virtue' to do so," writes historian Ortiz. "To the Anglo-American people, the lynching of Mexicans was not only expected, but was also promoted for the betterment of Anglo society."[9] White vigilantes were rarely arrested, and the few who were usually were acquitted at trial.

"The lynching of Mexicans . . . was based on the belief in the Anglo-American community that it was a 'civic virtue' to do so. To the Anglo-American people, the lynching of Mexicans was not only expected, but was also promoted for the betterment of Anglo society."[9]

—Camilo M. Ortiz, historian

The last publicly reported lynching of a Mexican American occurred in November 1928, when a drunken mob hung Rafael Benavides in Farmington, New Mexico. By this time, the federal government was beginning to take tentative steps to intervene in lynching cases when state officials failed to act. But communities that harbored a nativist bias soon found new ways to erase the presence of Hispanics.

Immigration and Deportation

Despite the threat of vigilante attacks, immigration by Hispanics increased during the early twentieth century. Driven from their

During the Great Depression, unemployed Americans vented their fear and anger on farmworkers from Mexico. Famed photographer Dorothea Lange captured this image of Mexican cotton pickers in South Texas in 1936.

homes in Mexico by political unrest, including a civil war, more than 680,000 Mexicans immigrated to the United States between 1910 and 1929. Most settled in the Southwest, where they worked in mines and on farms, ranches, and railroads.

When the United States entered World War I in 1917, millions of young Americans entered the armed forces, including many Hispanic Americans. In order to bolster the workforce, immigrants from Mexico were encouraged to fill the need for seasonal US farm labor. After the war ended, however, the US government began restricting immigration. The US Border Patrol was created in 1924 to control the movement of people across the US–Mexico border. Literacy tests and quota laws imposed in the 1920s slowed the flow of immigrants from Latin America.

The Great Depression of the 1930s brought greater discrimination against Hispanic Americans. Anglos were upset because

Hispanic or Latino?

Although the terms *Hispanic* and *Latino* (and even *Latinx*, an attempt at a gender-neutral term) are often used interchangeably, they actually have specific meanings. The English term *Latino* comes from the Spanish word *latinoamericano*, which refers to someone who is from Latin America (countries in the Americas where Spanish or Portuguese are the primary languages) or is descended from people who lived in Latin America. *Hispanic* is a broader term that refers to people who speak Spanish and/or are descended from any Spanish-speaking population. Thus, most Latinos (people from Latin America) are Hispanic, but so are people who live in or come from Spain, as well as Spanish speakers in other European countries, or are from Asia (e.g., Filipinos) or Africa (e.g., Western Saharans, Moroccans).

"Hispanic or Latino" is often used as a racial descriptor, similar to "white," "black," or "Asian." However, using "Hispanic or Latino" as a racial category is inaccurate because the populations this term describes are composed of diverse racial groups.

Mexican Americans had (low-paying) farm jobs while many "real" Americans were unemployed. Such complaints would create the conditions for a massive exodus, which began in 1930 as federal agents began raiding workplaces and arresting Hispanic workers. Thousands were deported with their families to Mexico, often without their possessions—including, in some cases, birth certificates proving they had been born in the United States. These raids created fear and uncertainty about the future in Hispanic communities.

Many towns and cities took advantage of this tension to rid their communities of Mexican Americans. Throughout the 1930s governments, businesses, and Anglo community leaders strongly encouraged (and in many cases, forced) Hispanic Americans to relocate to Mexico. State and local governments reduced or eliminated relief (welfare) payments to poor families, and employers warned Hispanic workers that they were likely to lose their jobs. Governments and civic organizations even paid the cost of train or bus transportation to the border as part of what was euphemistically called a "repatriation" program.

"Repatriation carries connotations that it is voluntary, that people are making their own decision without pressure to return to the country of their nationality," explains historian Francisco Balderrama. "But most obviously, how voluntary is it if you have deportation raids by the federal government during the [President Herbert] Hoover administration and people are disappearing on the streets? How voluntary is it if you have county agents knocking on people's doors telling people oh, you would be better off in Mexico and here are your train tickets? You should be ready to go in two weeks."[10]

Due to the combination of federal deportation policies and local repatriation programs, about 1 million Hispanics were forced out of the United States during the 1930s. Balderrama estimates that approximately 60 percent of them were US citizens—for them, the so-called repatriation moved them into a foreign country. Repatriation did not end until the 1940s, when World War II produced a shortage of workers for farms and wartime industries.

After the war, the federal government implemented a new series of deportation programs aimed at Mexican Americans. From 1954 to 1957, the US Immigration and Naturalization Service (INS) rounded up and deported about 1.3 million Mexican immigrants and their family members. Although INS programs were supposed to target illegal immigrants, American citizens were often deported as well, sometimes under appalling conditions. "Tens of thousands of immigrants were shoved into buses, boats and planes and sent to often-unfamiliar parts of Mexico, where they struggled to rebuild their lives," writes journalist Erin Blakemore. "In Chicago, three planes a week were filled with immigrants and flown to Mexico. In Texas, 25 percent of all of the immigrants deported were crammed onto boats later compared to slave ships, while others died of sunstroke, disease and other causes while in custody."[11]

The Hispanic Americans who remained in the United States experienced discrimination in many other ways. Restaurants could refuse to serve them, and they had to use the theaters, restrooms, swimming pools, and drinking fountains that were marked for "coloreds only." Schoolchildren were often punished in public schools for speaking Spanish. Hispanic farmworkers, in particular, had hard lives, with low pay, squalid living conditions, and few opportunities for their children to receive an education.

Fighting for a Place in America

Things would slowly start to improve for Hispanic Americans after World War II. Activists such as Reies Tijerina, Emma Tenayuca, and Hector Garcia, as well as organizations such as the American G.I. Forum, the National Council of La Raza (now called UnidosUS), the Mexican American Legal Defense and Educational Fund, and the United Farm Workers of America, fought to give Hispanics the same economic and civil rights and freedoms that other Americans enjoyed.

In 1954, the US Supreme Court ruled in *Hernandez v. Texas* that Hispanic American citizens were entitled to all the rights guaranteed in the Fourteenth Amendment. Additional court cases and legislation followed, culminating in the landmark achievements of the civil rights era: the 1964 Civil Rights Act and the 1965 Voting Rights Act. With these laws and others, the federal government finally committed to eliminating discrimination and the second-class citizen status of Hispanics and other minority groups.

Since the 1960s, the US Hispanic population has grown rapidly. The 1965 Immigration and Nationality Act eliminated the quota system that had been implemented during the 1920s, allowing more immigrants from Mexico and Latin America to enter the country. In 1965, Hispanics made up just 4 percent of the US population, but more than half of all immigrants since then have come from Latin America. Today, the US Census Bureau reports that more than 60 million Americans identify themselves

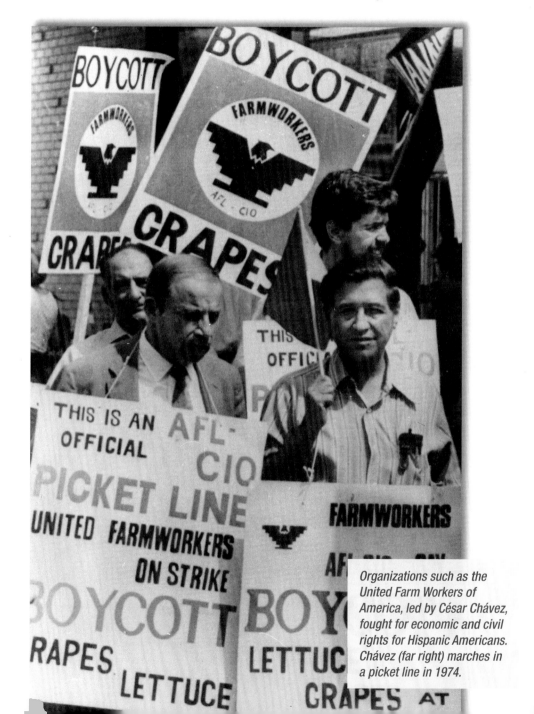

Organizations such as the United Farm Workers of America, led by César Chávez, fought for economic and civil rights for Hispanic Americans. Chávez (far right) marches in a picket line in 1974.

as Hispanic or Latino, a figure that represents more than 18 percent of the total US population and makes Hispanics the largest minority group in the United States.

During the twenty-first century, however, the rapid growth of the Hispanic population has created rising ambivalence among American citizens about future immigration. Some Americans are concerned about increased competition for jobs, especially during times when the nation's economy is not strong. "There is also an emotional dimension that shapes sentiments toward immigration," notes Charles Hirschman, a social demographer and professor at the University of Washington. He adds, "Many Americans, like people everywhere, are more comfortable with the familiar than with change. They fear that newcomers with different languages, religions, and cultures are reluctant to assimilate into American society and to learn English."[12]

Unfortunately, in recent years bigoted and unscrupulous political leaders and organizations have exploited fears about immigrants, especially those from Latin America, in order to gain or maintain political power.

CHAPTER TWO

Inciting Violence

In November 2019, after parking his truck outside a Mexican restaurant in a Milwaukee, Wisconsin, neighborhood, Mahud Villalaz, a forty-two-year-old Hispanic man, was confronted by sixty-one-year-old Clifton Blackwell, a white man. Blackwell berated Villalaz for parking too close to a bus stop, calling him an illegal immigrant. "Why did you invade my country. . . . Why don't you respect my laws?"[13] Blackwell angrily asked.

Villalaz, who in fact is an American citizen (he had immigrated legally from Peru in 2001 and was naturalized in 2013), attempted to defuse the situation by moving his truck to another parking spot, but Blackwell persisted. As Villalaz walked toward the restaurant hoping to avoid an unpleasant scene, Blackwell pointed at him and shouted, "Go back—go back."[14] Then he threw acid on Villalaz's face, causing serious burns to his face, cheek, and neck and injuring his left eye.

Such violent encounters involving Hispanic Americans have, unfortunately, become more common since about 2015, as anti-immigrant groups and politicians have angrily denounced immigrants and asylum seekers from Latin America. Their bitter attacks have inspired a wave of violence aimed at Hispanics; for example, just two days after the November 2016 presidential election, a white Florida man was arrested for attacking a Hispanic man outside a Gainesville convenience store. According to police, a surveillance video recorded twenty-three-year-old Caleb Illig attacking Pablo

Echevarria, who was cleaning the parking lot around 1:00 a.m. Illig punched Echevarria repeatedly in the back of the head while yelling, "This is for Donald Trump."[15]

Later, in April 2018, a black man wearing a red hat with "Make America Great Again" on the front started an argument with a twenty-four-year-old Hispanic man on a Manhattan subway train. Following the Hispanic man off the train, the attacker punched him in the head and shoved him onto the train tracks, then escaped into the crowd of commuters.

Then, a few months later, two New Orleans police officers, Spencer Sutton and John Galman, were fired from their jobs and faced criminal charges for beating up Jorge Alberto Gomez, a US citizen and military veteran, outside a bar on July 24, 2018. The two officers, both under age twenty-five, were off duty at the time. "They kept telling me I wasn't an American citizen, that I was a fake American,"[16] Gomez told the *New Orleans Advocate*. Sutton and Galman were both fired from the police force but received suspended prison sentences as part of a plea bargain that included paying Gomez a total of $10,000 in restitution.

> "They kept telling me I wasn't an American citizen, that I was a fake American."[16]
>
> —Jorge Alberto Gomez, anti-immigration attack victim

Nativism on the Campaign Trail

The attacks seemed to reflect a bias against Hispanics, and some political analysts believe this attitude was stoked by political rhetoric circulating at the time. Soon after he launched his presidential campaign in 2015, candidate Donald Trump began portraying most immigrants from Mexico as "rapists," "animals," and "predators" who brought drugs, crime, and other problems across the border. He described the arrival of refugees from Central America as an "invasion" and promised to defend America by building a border wall. Even Trump's campaign slogan can be seen as including a coded dig at immigrants. "Make America Great Again" ap-

Donald Trump campaigns for president in 2015. Hostility toward Hispanics was stoked, some say, by Trump's depictions of immigrants from Mexico as rapists, animals, and predators.

pears to be a straightforward, patriotic call to action—the sort of thing that many politicians have promised over the years. But adding the word *again* subtly changes the slogan's meaning, making it a commitment to return the United States to an earlier time. Following Trump's campaign statements as well as his actions as president, his critics maintain that it is easy to infer that the supposedly bygone "great" era was one in which white culture was dominant and there were fewer nonwhite immigrants.

Many historians have pointed out that Trump's campaign language vilifying Hispanics and other immigrants is very similar to the rhetoric used during previous periods in American history when nativists were angry about high levels of immigration. During the 1840s and 1850s, for example, the secretive Know Nothing Party described immigrants as "liars, villains, and cowardly cutthroats" and promised to "keep America for the Americans."[17] From the 1890s to the 1920s, groups like the Immigration Restriction League characterized immigrants from southern and eastern

Hispanics Who Support Trump

Many observers believe Donald Trump has consistently insulted and denigrated immigrants from Latin America and pursued too-restrictive immigration policies as president. Yet in January 2020, a poll by the Marist Institute for Public Opinion found that 50 percent of Hispanic respondents approved of the job Trump was doing as president. Thirty percent said they intended to vote for the Republican incumbent in the fall election.

Though Hispanic support for Trump may seem surprising, it reflects the community's diversity. Most Hispanics in California, Texas, and other southwestern states are of Mexican descent. Florida is home to many Cuban Americans. Puerto Ricans and Dominicans predominate in the northeastern states of New York and New Jersey. These groups have different experiences and interests. Some have lived in the United States for so long that they no longer identify with their ancestral culture. Others want to see the door closed to future immigrants for economic reasons. And some disagree with the Democratic Party on social issues, such as abortion or gay marriage, due to their Roman Catholic or evangelical religious beliefs.

"When Democrats reach out to Latino voters, they are too focused on immigration, and say too little about other issues these voters prioritize," explains Kristian Ramos, a former communications director for the Congressional Hispanic Caucus. "If they want to win over enough Latino votes to retake the White House, Democrats must continue to fight for the immigrant community, but they must also offer a positive, aspirational narrative that embraces Latinos as a vibrant part of America."

Kristian Ramos, "Latino Support for Trump Is Real," *The Atlantic*, February 17, 2020. www.theatlantic.com.

Europe, such as Italians and Poles, as "generally undesirable," describing them as "unintelligent, of low vitality, of poor physique . . . and unfitted mentally or morally for good citizenship."[18]

Trump's campaign comments angered and offended many Hispanic Americans but energized conservative, anti-immigration groups that had been criticizing the system for years. During the presidential campaign, conservative talk radio hosts promoted the "Great Replacement" theory, speculating that the Democratic Party was encouraging greater immigration as part of a plot to systematically replace whites in America with people of color, who would presumably vote Democratic.

Trump's words also caught the ear of political extremists, collectively referred to as the alt-right, who want to establish white supremacy in the United States. Believing that his policies aligned with their interests, these white supremacist groups were more than happy to attack Trump's political opponents on his behalf. In early 2016, a political action committee associated with the white supremacist American Freedom Party distributed a robocall (machine-dialed, prerecorded phone call) in several states prior to their Republican primary elections. The call targeted Marco Rubio and Ted Cruz, US senators from Florida and Texas, respectively, who are Cuban American and who, like Trump, were seeking the Republican Party's presidential nomination. "The white race is dying out in America and Europe because we are afraid to be called 'racist,'" said the call. "Donald Trump is not a racist, but Donald Trump is not afraid. Don't vote for a Cuban. Vote for Donald Trump."[19]

During and after the campaign, Trump occasionally spoke out against the hateful messages of white supremacists, although he never forcefully condemned such groups. He contended that his words were being misconstrued or taken out of context. "I am the least racist person that you have ever met,"[20] Trump claimed in a December 2015 interview with CNN's Don Lemon. Many commentators, however, believe that Trump's deliberate use of certain words and terms, along with his constant verbal assaults on immigrants and Hispanics, sent a clear signal to the alt-right that he agreed with and supported their racist worldview. "Many of [Trump's] statements are exactly what a white supremacist would say—whether talking about immigrants invading . . . or [that] Mexicans are rapists," explains Heidi Beirich, a director of the Southern Poverty Law Center, which tracks the activities of hate groups and extremist organizations in the United States. She notes that Trump has "tweeted out material that came from white supremacists, and a lot of his views are indirectly views from white nationalists. I don't know if that makes him a white nationalist, but he's talking from their scripts. There is a link between this kind of rhetoric and violence."[21]

That link was clearly demonstrated prior to the presidential election, when brothers Scott and Steve Leader were arrested in Boston in August 2015 for beating a Hispanic immigrant with a pipe and then urinating on him. "Donald Trump was right," the two men said, according to police. "All these illegals need to be deported."[22] (The victim was working in the country legally.) When told about the incident, Trump said it was "terrible" but also made an excuse for the white attackers' violence. "I will say, the people that are following me are very passionate," Trump said. "They love this country; they want this country to be great again."[23]

> "Many of [Trump's] statements are exactly what a white supremacist would say—whether talking about immigrants invading . . . or [that] Mexicans are rapists. . . . There is a link between this kind of rhetoric and violence."[21]
>
> —Heidi Beirich, Southern Poverty Law Center

Inciting Violence as President

Since being elected president in November 2016, Trump has worked to enact the anti-immigration policies he promised while campaigning. He has insisted on constructing a wall at the US–Mexico border, increased deportations, sharply reduced the numbers of refugees admitted into the United States, and tried to eliminate the Deferred Action for Childhood Arrivals program, which protects young people who were brought into the country illegally when they were children from deportation.

During 2017 and 2018, Trump regularly called attention to so-called migrant caravans, large groups of refugees traveling together from Central America to the southern border of the United States, seeking asylum. He claimed that terrorists and drug dealers were using these caravans to sneak into the United States. "This is an invasion of our Country and our Military is waiting for you,"[24] Trump warned. His words inspired anger toward Hispanic immigrants among some of his supporters, and they resolved to do something about it. Considering Trump's message to be a call to action, numerous armed paramilitary groups such as the Arizona Border Recon, the United Constitutional Patriots, and the Minutemen headed to Texas and Arizona. Wearing camouflage and often equipped with night-vision goggles and semiautomatic AR-15 rifles, these groups vowed to help federal troops and the US Border Patrol resist the "invasion."

Members of militia groups often believe they are acting in the spirit of previous generations of American patriots; however, federal authorities and many independent observers consider these civilians to be vigilantes who want to take a government responsibility—the duty to protect the border—into their own hands. In this sense, they are little better than the lynch mobs in the Southwest in the nineteenth century. The US Department of Defense estimates that at least two hundred armed militia members were active at the border, intercepting border crossers and holding them at gunpoint until US Customs and Border Protection (CBP) officers could arrive.

Hondurans fleeing poverty and violence board a truck in 2018 in Oaxaca, Mexico. As president, Trump repeatedly described the people in the Central American migrant caravans as invaders.

"What's troubling is, what you see today, the forms of vigilante violence like policing the border, they are responding to the rhetoric by state and federal officials who are stoking fear," comments Monica Muñoz Martinez, author of *The Injustice Never Leaves You: Anti-Mexican Violence in Texas*. She warns that "the racist rhetoric, focusing specifically on people who are Latino, creates a public acceptance of violent border policing and nativist immigration policies."[25]

A Growing Sense of Fear

During the Trump presidency, many Hispanics have said they feel concerned and uncertain about their future in America due to anxiety about both his words and his actions. In a 2019 survey by the Pew Hispanic Center, 75 percent of immigrants who were not yet US citizens said that the president's rhetoric made them feel unsafe. But even Hispanics whose families have lived in the United States for generations said that they are unsettled by Trump's hard-line policies. More than half of these longtime Americans said that they are afraid for their families' safety. "The climate of fear is heightened more than I've ever seen it in my life,"[26] commented Irene Sanchez, a Mexican American citizen who teaches school in Los Angeles.

After the August 2019 El Paso shooting, "many Latinos expressed fear that two main external indicators [that one is Latino]—the brownness of one's skin and the use of Spanish in public—might trigger people to physically attack them,"[27] noted Graciela Mochkofsky, an immigrant from Argentina who is the director of the Spanish-language journalism program at City University of New York.

In a *New Yorker* essay, Mochkofsky describes several unsettling encounters that she has experienced since Trump's election. In one incident, a white coworker casually mentioned that the police might one day be looking to arrest her son, who was just

"What you see today, the forms of vigilante violence like policing the border, they are responding to the rhetoric by state and federal officials who are stoking fear."[25]

—Monica Muñoz Martinez, historian and author

28

Skin Color and Discrimination

The term *Hispanic* refers to an ethnicity, not a race. There were few white European women in Spain's New World colonies during the seventeenth and eighteenth centuries, so Spanish settlers often intermarried with Native Americans. Their mixed-race descendants were known as *mestizos*. African slaves brought to work in New Spain added another racial dimension to this cultural heritage. Due to this blending of people, Hispanic Americans today have a wide range of skin colors, from white to brown to black.

Hispanic Americans are not excluded from the long history of discrimination against people of color in the United States. Among all Hispanic American adults, 58 percent say they have been treated unfairly because of their ethnicity at some time in the past year. A 2019 Pew Research Center survey determined that Hispanics with darker skin were more likely to experience discrimination (64 percent) than those with lighter skin (50 percent). Overall, Hispanics with darker skin are more likely to say that others have treated them as if they were not very intelligent (55 percent, compared to 36 percent of lighter-skinned Hispanics), acted suspicious of them (43 percent to 27 percent), or subjected them to racial slurs or offensive jokes (53 percent to 34 percent). Darker-skinned Hispanics are also more likely to be stopped by police (24 percent to 11 percent). Notes Pew researcher Ana Gonzalez-Barrera, "These differences in experiences with discrimination hold even after controlling for characteristics such as gender, age, education and whether they were born in the U.S. or abroad."

Ana Gonzalez-Barrera, "Hispanics with Darker Skin Are More Likely to Experience Discrimination than Those with Lighter Skin," Pew Research Center, July 2, 2019. www.pewresearch.org.

seven years old at the time. In another, Mochkofsky was speaking Spanish to her son in a bakery when she noticed the young woman behind the counter giving her a confused look. "For a fraction of a second, a freezing shiver ran down my spine, and I lowered my voice," wrote Mochkofsky. "Then she explained that she couldn't place where we were from, and asked us. I had made a wrong assumption, but the fear I felt was real."[28]

The Price of Hateful Language

A more serious incident took place on July 28, 2019, when a white teenager named Santino Legan sneaked into an outdoor food festival in Gilroy, California, a community where almost 60 percent of the residents are Hispanic. Armed with a semiautomatic AK-47-style rifle, Legan opened fire on the crowd. He fired thirty-nine shots, killing two Hispanic children (a thirteen-year-old girl and a six-year-old boy) and a twenty-five-year-old black man. Legan wounded seventeen others during the rampage before being shot several times by local police; he took his own life before being apprehended.

In the aftermath, it appeared Legan had intentionally targeted nonwhites. Although he did not leave any note or manifesto explaining his reasons, shortly before the attack, Legan, whose stated ancestry was Italian and Iranian, had posted a derogatory comment about "mestizos" (an archaic term originally applied to those of mixed European and Native American heritage) on social media. In the same post he encouraged his online followers to read a book written by a white supremacist. But the attack was soon overshadowed in the media by an even deadlier assault less

Gilroy residents attend a vigil for victims of the July 2019 mass shooting at the town's annual Garlic Festival. On social media, the shooter used derogatory language and promoted a book written by a white supremacist.

than a week later, when Patrick Crusius used a similar weapon to kill twenty-two people in El Paso, Texas.

Responding to these attacks, Trump finally spoke unequivocally to tamp down the violence. "In one voice, our nation must condemn racism, bigotry and white supremacy," he said in a speech from the White House. "These sinister ideologies must be defeated. Hate has no place in America."[29]

Most Americans agree with these remarks; however, they also say that the threatening and divisive language that political leaders, including Trump, have used to target Hispanics is not appropriate. Eighty-five percent of Americans told the Pew Research Center in 2019 that political debate has become more negative and less respectful in recent years. Fifty-five percent of respondents blamed Trump for making the tone and nature of debate worse. Almost 80 percent of Americans said that public officials should not use angry or aggressive language to demonize members of racial, religious, or ethnic groups because it makes violence against those groups more likely.

Although the president tried to reach out to Hispanics in the wake of the El Paso shooting, many said his attempt to calm the situation was coming much too late. Local community leaders, as well as the families of the victims, said that the president should not come to their city to express his sympathy. When he persisted, hundreds of people showed up to protest his arrival, carrying signs that read "Not Welcome Here" and "Racist Go Home."

"He should not come here while we are in mourning," said Representative Veronica Escobar, whose district includes El Paso. "Words have consequences," she added, "and the president has made my community and my people the enemy. He has told the country that we are people to be feared, people to be hated."[30]

Unfortunately, many Hispanic Americans remain fearful about living in the United States due to the divisive language of the current era. "Every day when I take my daughter to school we pray. I ask God to protect her," says Lidia Carrillo, who has lived in the United States for more than thirty years. "I don't know if I'm going to see my daughter or my husband at the end of the day."[31]

CHAPTER THREE

The Language of America

In May 2018, two young Hispanic nurses were detained by a CBP officer after he overheard them speaking Spanish in a convenience store in Havre, Montana. Ana Suda and Martha Hernandez are US citizens who work together at a medical clinic and were both born in the United States. Hernandez had lived in Havre for eight years, while Suda had lived there for five years. The two women were speaking together while in line to purchase groceries when they were interrupted by CBP agent Paul O'Neal. He asked them for identification and refused to allow them to leave until he could check their immigration status.

The two women were detained for about thirty-five minutes. During this time, Suda recorded a portion of her conversation with O'Neal. When she asked why they had been stopped, O'Neal explained, "It's the fact that it has to do with you guys speaking Spanish in the store, in a state where it's predominantly English-speaking, OK?"[32] Eventually, when their documentation checked out, Suda and Hernandez were permitted to leave.

Angry and humiliated, Suda decided to post her video of the encounter on YouTube and Facebook. She later explained that her motivation to make the encounter public was to "instill pride in her daughter for being bilingual—to show her that, in spite of what had happened to her mother, she should not be afraid of using Spanish in public."[33] The video soon went viral.

In February 2019, the American Civil Liberties Union (ACLU), an organization that helps US citizens stand up for their rights, helped Suda and Hernandez file a lawsuit ordering the CBP not to stop or detain anyone simply for speaking Spanish. Because Havre is only about 20 miles (32 km) from the Canadian border, both English and French are commonly heard in the small town. In fact, the lawsuit noted that O'Neal had told the women that they would not have been stopped if they had been conversing in French. It was their Spanish-language conversation that triggered his intervention. "The incident itself is troubling enough because they were engaged in utterly normal conduct that you and I do on a daily basis, shopping at the grocery store or shopping at the convenience store, and they were pulled aside in that situation and we believe that's simply unconstitutional,"[34] comments Alex Rate, the legal director of the ACLU's Montana branch.

After posting the video of the encounter and filing the federal lawsuit, Suda and Hernandez were harassed by some of their neighbors. After a few months, both women moved away from the community. "I can't take it anymore," Suda says. "Our lives are not the same; it's not the same anymore. These guys destroyed everything we have. . . . They destroyed my life, but if I can help somebody else with this speaking out, I'll take it."[35] Unfortunately, the story of Ana Suda and Martha Hernandez is not an isolated case.

"This Is America—Speak English"

For decades, Hispanics in the United States have reported being abused and harassed for speaking Spanish in public. The Pew Research Center reports that more than one in five Hispanics say that they have been criticized for speaking Spanish, often with a variation of the phrase "This is America—speak English," or told to go back to their home country. For example, in 2018 a video of Aaron Schlossberg, a wealthy Manhattan attorney, berating Spanish-speaking restaurant employees went viral, and in July 2019, two white women told Ricardo Castillo, a US citizen of Puerto

Hispanics Face Discrimination

Thirty-eight percent of Hispanics in the United States said they had experienced bias or personal attacks because of their ethnicity, according to a recent Pew Research Center survey. The survey asked about four types of offensive incidents: experiencing unfair treatment or bias; being criticized for speaking Spanish in public; being told to go back to their home country; and being called offensive names. Additionally, the survey found that recent immigrants were more likely to experience discrimination than those whose families had lived in the United States for three or more generations. One bright spot in the survey was the response from 37 percent who said they had received expressions of support from other individuals.

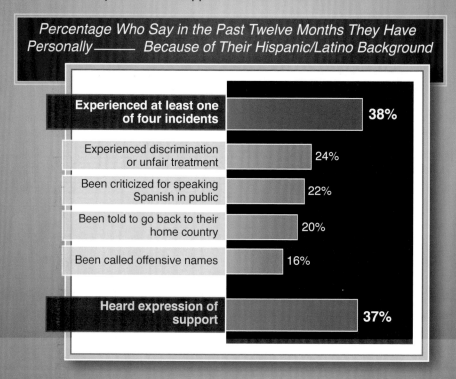

Percentage Who Say in the Past Twelve Months They Have Personally _____ Because of Their Hispanic/Latino Background

Experienced at least one of four incidents	38%
Experienced discrimination or unfair treatment	24%
Been criticized for speaking Spanish in public	22%
Been told to go back to their home country	20%
Been called offensive names	16%
Heard expression of support	37%

Source: Mark Hugo Lopez, Ana Gonzales-Barrera, and Jens Manuel Krogstad, "More Latinos Have Serious Concerns About Their Place in America Under Trump," Pew Research Center, October 25, 2018. ww.pewresearch.org.

Rican descent who manages a Florida fast-food restaurant, "Go back to Mexico if you want to keep speaking Spanish."[36] In February 2020, Adrian Iraola, a Mexican immigrant who has been a US citizen for nearly four decades, was speaking at a Michigan school board meeting about ehtnically motivated bullying of his child when a member of the audience insultingly asked why he did not return to Mexico if he was unsatisfied with America.

Many Spanish-speaking Americans have reported similar incidents stemming from the use of Spanish in the workplace. "Once, while at work, I asked a Hispanic girl to let me know when she went to lunch so that I could join her," comments one sixty-six-year-old woman. She spoke to her friend in Spanish, which apparently upset her supervisor. "I immediately got called to personnel and was told to please speak English and that people were getting nervous. I asked if it was a rule and she said, 'No, we prefer you speak English.' I quit the second time I was called to personnel. I said there are plenty of jobs out there and I don't have to deal with this."[37]

In the United States, the issue of language has been controversial for many years, but many Hispanics' discomfort has increased since Trump's election. "The attacks that we now see on people who speak Spanish were already happening before," says Heidi Beirich of the Southern Poverty Law Center. "But when you are the subject of such an attack and you know that millions of people share your attacker's vision, including the president of the United States, you feel much more vulnerable."[38]

> "The attacks that we now see on people who speak Spanish were already happening before. But when you are the subject of such an attack and you know that millions of people share your attacker's vision, including the president of the United States, you feel much more vulnerable."[38]
>
> —Heidi Beirich, Southern Poverty Law Center

Land of Many Languages

Unlike many other countries, the United States has never established an official language. Since 1776, English has been the predominant language of the United States, but throughout history immigrants have arrived speaking a variety of other languages. Today, more than 65 million Americans speak a language other than English or are bilingual, according to the US Census Bureau's American Community Survey. Although Americans speak several hundred different languages, Spanish speakers are the largest group, at more than 40 million.

Nativists argue that the continued use of other languages by immigrants is a sign that they are not willing to become "fully

Multilingualism and Politics

The issue of language came up during a Democratic Party debate held in February 2020 in Nevada, a state where Hispanics make up more than 27 percent of the population. During the debate, former South Bend, Indiana, mayor Pete Buttigieg criticized fellow debater Minnesota senator Amy Klobuchar for supporting legislation in 2007 that would have ended a requirement for federal agencies to provide materials in languages other than English. "You voted to make English the national language," Buttigieg said. "Do you know what message that sends in as multilingual a state as Nevada to immigrants?"

Buttigieg was referring to a vote taken in the US Senate during June 2007 on an amendment to legislation that was intended to reform the immigration system. Proposed by Republican senator James M. Inhofe of Oklahoma, the amendment declared English to be the national language, required new immigrants to pass an English proficiency test, and largely eliminated federal requirements for providing non-English services. The amendment passed easily, 64–33, with the support of both Democrats and Republicans. However, the Comprehensive Immigration Reform Act was never passed by Congress, so the Inhofe amendment never went into effect.

Klobuchar had previously disavowed her 2007 vote while campaigning in Las Vegas, saying that she had changed her stance on the issue. Klobuchar told reporters that she believes English-only laws no longer make sense in "a country like ours that is so diverse."

Quoted in Ewan Palmer, "Amy Klobuchar Refuses to Shake Pete Buttigieg's Hand After Clashing Repeatedly During Nevada Debate," *Newsweek*, February 20, 2020. www.newsweek.com.

American" by assimilating into the culture in the same way that previous generations of immigrants did. Several organizations, such as ProEnglish and US English, were formed to address this concern. These groups advocate for English to become the official language of the United States. "Official English would . . . reinforce America's historic message to new immigrants—that we expect them to learn English as the first step in their assimilation—

and that we are committed to ensuring that all Americans share in the economic, social and political benefits of having a common language,"[39] writes K.C. McAlpin, the former executive director of ProEnglish. Nativists also point out that immigrants who can speak and understand English are more likely to succeed in the United States, both economically and socially.

Even those who are sympathetic and supportive of immigrants recognize and agree that this second point is accurate; however, they also tend to believe that Spanish speakers do not threaten the primacy of the English language in the United States. English is the dominant language used for business and communication, not just in America but around the world. Most immigrants eventually learn to speak passable English, and their children nearly always become fluent in the language. The Pew Research Center reports that 90 percent of Hispanics born in the United States are proficient in English. Although the English proficiency rate is considerably lower among foreign-born Latinos, at 36 percent, Pew found that, overall, 70 percent of all Hispanic Americans over age five are proficient in English.

"Although the United States doesn't legally mandate an 'official' language, English is the *de facto* language of the land," writes *Washington Post* columnist Christopher Ingraham. He explains that

> people who lack English proficiency may face all manner of social, educational and economic roadblocks as they attempt to navigate society. However, the census data show that more than 60 percent of citizen and noncitizen US residents who speak other languages at home also speak English "very well." They're bilingual, in other words, and speaking other languages out of choice, not necessity.[40]

> "Official English would . . . reinforce America's historic message to new immigrants—that we expect them to learn English as the first step in their assimilation."[39]
>
> —K.C. McAlpin, former executive director of ProEnglish

A Linguistic Double Standard

Ironically, for white Americans, being multilingual can be highly beneficial. The ability to speak a second language can open new career opportunities, and studies have found that bilingual speakers process information more efficiently and more easily than people who know a single language. Unlike Ana Suda, Martha Hernandez, and other Spanish-speaking workers, white American politicians, businesspeople, and entertainers are often praised for trying to speak Spanish in public, even haltingly. "It is a deficit when [Hispanics] speak Spanish, but it's an asset to whites and white Americans when they speak it," observes educator and author Nicole Gonzalez Van Cleve. "This is the ultimate form of exclusion."[41]

Some Hispanic Americans say they prefer not to speak Spanish in public because they fear others will view them as uneducated or as a recent immigrant. The Pew Research Center found that although 97 percent of immigrants from Latin America speak Spanish to their children at home, just 71 percent of Hispanics born in America to an immigrant parent speak Spanish to their own children at home. The trend continues the longer they are in America—just 49 percent of third-generation Americans (people whose grandparent was an immigrant) speak Spanish to their children at home. Although most Hispanics say that the Spanish language is an important element of their culture, Pew found that 20 percent of Hispanics actively discouraged their children from speaking Spanish—often because of discrimination that they experienced in America, such as being punished for speaking Spanish in school.

When she was looking for a running mate during her 2016 presidential campaign, Hillary Clinton considered two Hispanic members of President Barack Obama's cabinet: Secretary of Housing and Urban Development Julián Castro and Secretary of Labor Thomas Perez. However, Clinton ultimately chose Tim

"It is a deficit when [Hispanics] speak Spanish, but it's an asset to whites and white Americans when they speak it. This is the ultimate form of exclusion."[41]

—Nicole Gonzalez Van Cleve, educator and author

Kaine, a white senator from Virginia, as the Democratic Party's vice presidential candidate. Clinton's aides explained that she chose Kaine in part because he was more comfortable than either Castro or Perez about giving speeches in Spanish.

Many people were disappointed and frustrated with Clinton's decision to pass over the two highly qualified candidates for such a shallow reason. "I was looking for a VP choice that showed my son that one day he could be president—not that he needs to work on his Spanish,"[42] commented Chuck Rocha, a third-generation Mexican American from Texas and a Democratic political consultant. Others criticized news reports that implied Castro and Perez were somehow less effective as politicians because they prefer to communicate in English, although both men can speak Spanish. A survey by the Spanish-language television station Univision found that only 26 percent of viewers said their vote would be influenced by whether a person spoke Spanish, while 68 percent said it would not. The voters who were surveyed were much more concerned with a candidate's positions on issues like immigration and the economy.

"This is a textbook example of a raciolinguistic ideology," writes Nelson Flores, a linguistics professor at the University of Pennsylvania. "For a white politician, it is an asset to have any Spanish-speaking abilities. For a Latinx politician, it is a liability not to have perfect Spanish-speaking abilities. This stance is particularly ironic for a society that has at many points actually worked to undermine the bilingualism of the Latinx community."[43]

Legislative Actions

Since the 1960s, the federal government has made significant efforts to accommodate non-English speakers. In the 1974 case *Lau v. Nichols*, the US Supreme Court ruled that public schools had to educate students in their native language if they could not speak English proficiently. Later that year, Congress passed the Equal Educational Opportunities Act, which—among other things—required schools to eliminate language barriers that kept non-English-speaking students from participating in classes taught in English.

Court decisions throughout the 1980s supported this legislation, requiring state education departments to comply with the federal mandates and create bilingual education programs for students who were learning to speak English. Today, nearly all public schools offer English as a second language (ESL) programs for students who qualify, as well as English-immersion programs designed to help English language learners make a successful transition into English-language classrooms.

Similarly, in 1975 the Voting Rights Act was amended to require election officials to provide multilingual ballots or language assistance in polling places where more than ten thousand voting-age citizens, or at least 5 percent of the voting district's population, are not proficient in English. Under the Civil Rights Act of 1964, hospitals and medical

Middle school students in Tennessee celebrate the completion of their school's ESL program in 2018. Many public schools offer such programs to help immigrants successfully transition into US society.

Critical Coronavirus Communication

In the spring of 2020, the spread of coronavirus (or COVID-19), an infectious virus that causes respiratory illnesses, resulted in a shutdown of schools, businesses, sports leagues, and public gatherings nationwide. Public health officials with the Centers for Disease Control and Prevention (CDC) and other agencies worked to keep people informed about the new virus and how to prevent it from spreading. On Monday, March 16, the federal government released guidelines intended to slow the spread of COVID-19.

The news media soon pointed out that the information, posted on the CDC's website as well as the White House website, was only available in English. By Wednesday, March 18, simple translations of some information into Spanish and Chinese were posted on both sites; however, links to many resources were not translated. Also, over the next week. Spanish-language public service announcements tended to appear a few days after the English-language announcements.

Hispanic leaders were concerned that Spanish speakers would be at greater risk of contracting the virus if they did not receive information in a timely fashion. "Our federal government has a responsibility to ensure that everyone in our communities—whether they speak English, Spanish, or any other language—has access to the same public health information on the coronavirus crisis," said Representative Joaquín Castro of Texas, the chair of the Congressional Hispanic Caucus.

J. Edward Moreno and Raphael Bernal, "Language Barriers Hamper Coronavirus Response," *The Hill* (Washington, DC), March 22, 2020. https://thehill.com.

clinics are required to ensure equal treatment of people who are not proficient in English by providing translation services and materials in their native language. And federal laws also prohibit unfair or deceptive acts or practices in interstate commerce, including false advertising practices intended to confuse Americans who have a limited understanding of English. Government agencies like the Office of Fair Housing and Equal Opportunity and the US Equal

Employment Opportunity Commission were created to ensure that this legislation is consistently enforced.

Nativist reaction to the civil rights legislation, as well as increased immigration from Latin America since 1965, resulted in a reemergence of an English-only movement. The movement had originated during the early twentieth century, but nativists at that time were mainly concerned about the influx of Jewish, Italian, and Slavic immigrants from southern, central, and eastern Europe. During the 1980s, chiefly in response to Spanish speakers, organizations like ProEnglish and US English were established to advocate for English-only laws at the federal and state government levels.

To date, English-only efforts have failed at the national level. Most recently, the English Language Unity Act has been introduced in several sessions of Congress since 2005 (most recently in 2017). If passed into law, the act would make English the official language of the United States. Although the legislation was considered by both the House of Representatives and the Senate in 2017, it did not advance beyond committee discussion in either chamber.

Symbolic Language Laws

Although there remains no official US language, as of 2020 thirty-two states had passed legislation establishing English as their official language. The most recent was West Virginia, which passed a law in March 2016 requiring all official state, county, and local government business to be conducted in English. Like most state language laws, however, West Virginia's legislation includes a number of exceptions. In West Virginia and most other states, governments can provide information on matters of public health and safety in languages other than English as needed or promote economic development, commerce, or tourism to non-English speakers. Election materials and state examinations for licensing drivers or skilled workers can also be provided in another language, so long as the English-language test is also offered. And law-enforcement officials are permitted to speak Spanish or other languages as needed for criminal investigations.

Despite laws that prohibit English-only policies in most businesses, one Philadelphia restaurant owner posted signs asking patrons to use English when ordering. He was cited for possible violation of a city ordinance.

State language laws are mainly symbolic, as it turns out. State and local governments must still comply with all federal mandates related to education, voting, health care, and commerce. And it would be nearly impossible for any workplace or public place to impose an English-only policy that does not violate federal antidiscrimination statutes. "These official English laws appear on their face to have little more [legal] significance than a state's choice of an official motto or the official state bird,"[44] writes Steven Bender, associate dean of the Seattle University School of Law.

CHAPTER FOUR

Dealing with Discrimination

The United States has changed in fundamental ways since the civil rights movement of the 1960s. Today, federal laws like the 1964 Civil Rights Act and the 1968 Fair Housing Act prohibit discrimination due to a person's race, color, gender, age, religion, or national origin. Federal laws also prevent harassment, such as offensive or derogatory remarks, based on these characteristics. The major legal and social reforms implemented during the civil rights movement of the 1960s and 1970s reduced some of the barriers that hindered Hispanics and other minority groups from achieving educational and economic success in America.

By the early twenty-first century, increasing numbers of Hispanics were moving into the American middle class, and schools and businesses were promoting the benefits of inclusion and diversity. These led some Americans, mostly whites, to conclude that antidiscrimination laws and affirmative action programs had successfully cleared the way for Hispanics and other racial minorities to overcome the effects of past inequality. Many pundits predicted in November 2008 that the election of Barack Obama as president would usher in a postracial era—a time when racial discrimination was essentially nonexistent and all Americans were treated equally.

That postracial society has yet to exist. According to a 2017 survey conducted for National Public Radio, the Robert Wood Johnson Foundation, and Harvard University's T.H. Chan School of Public Health, Hispanic Americans, despite federal laws and programs to eliminate discrimination, continue to encounter significant discrimination in many aspects of their lives. This includes in the workplace, where 33 percent of Hispanic Americans surveyed said they did not get a job because of their race or they were paid less than white workers for doing the same job.

Other research confirms this observation. A 2017 review by Northwestern University sociologist Lincoln Quillian and colleagues of twenty-five years of job hiring data found that white job applicants, on average, were 24 percent more likely to be hired or called back for a second interview than were Hispanics. "Contrary to claims of declining discrimination in American society," the researchers concluded, "our estimates suggest that levels of discrimination remain largely unchanged, at least at the point of hire."[45]

President Lyndon Johnson signs the Civil Rights Act into law on July 2, 1964. This federal law prohibits discrimination based on race, skin color, gender, age, religion, or national origin.

Discrimination in the Workplace

Discrimination in hiring has a broader effect than simply blocking one person from getting a job. Over time, it effectively suppresses the wages of the entire group of workers. The lower rate of second-interview callbacks and job offers found in the 2017 study means that Hispanic workers tend to have fewer job offers to choose from. This gives them less leverage to negotiate a higher salary or a better package of benefits when they do accept a position. Essentially, in other words, they must accept whatever they are offered.

Consequently, wage discrimination is an ongoing and widespread problem. The US Department of Labor has found that Hispanic workers earn 15 percent less than white workers doing the same job. The gap is wider among college-educated men, with Hispanics earning 20 percent less than whites on average. The 11 million Hispanic women in the American workforce are even more affected by wage discrimination. In every occupation, Hispanic women earn less than white women, and much less than white men. According to a 2020 study by the National Partnership for Women and Families, Hispanic women are paid 46 percent less, on average, than white men doing the same job, and 31 percent less than white women.

"Latinas are typically paid just 54 cents for every dollar paid to white, non-Hispanic men," reports the National Partnership for Women and Families. "The median annual pay for a Latina in the United States who holds a full-time, year-round job is $33,540, while the median annual pay for a white, non-Hispanic man who holds a full-time, year-round job is $61,576—a difference of $28,036 per year,"[46] the partnership asserts. That is a significant difference in wages; it means that Hispanic women have less money to support themselves and their families, as well as less to save or invest for the future.

> "Latinas are typically paid just 54 cents for every dollar paid to white, non-Hispanic men."[46]
>
> —National Partnership for Women and Families

46

Migrant farmworkers pick and package strawberries in Central California. Overall, Hispanics are more likely to be employed in labor-intensive, low-paid industries such as agriculture.

This gender wage gap persists even in the highest-paid occupations. US Census Bureau statistics show that the median pay for female Hispanic chief executives is around $71,000 per year, compared to about $109,000 for white men. Hispanic women who are computer scientists are paid about $25,000 a year less, on average, than non-Hispanic white men.

Overall, Hispanics are less likely to work in white-collar professions (which offer higher salaries) and more likely to be employed in labor-intensive industries such as construction or agriculture, which pay lower average wages across the board. This is because Hispanics have fewer opportunities for higher education or skills training. Studies show that Hispanics, and particularly immigrants, have historically been underrepresented in colleges and other institutions of higher education. As of 2020, just 16

Dolores Huerta

For most of the twentieth century, migrant farmworkers in Texas, California, and other states endured terrible living and working conditions. Often, the Hispanic migrants worked ten or more hours a day in the hot sun, seven days a week, earning just 15 cents an hour for backbreaking labor. They lived in shacks or tents that did not have running water or electricity, and health care was practically nonexistent.

During the 1960s, a young Mexican American woman named Dolores Huerta sought to improve the living and working conditions for migrant farmworkers. In 1962, she helped activist César Chávez establish a union that would eventually become known as the United Farm Workers of America. In 1965, Huerta assisted in organizing a strike against grape growers in Delano County, California, to draw attention to the challenges that workers faced. This protest evolved into a nation-wide grape boycott that lasted five years, ending when California farm owners agreed to provide higher wages and better housing to their migrant workers. Huerta negotiated that agreement. Over the next twenty years, she also partici-pated in many other labor actions and advocated for state and federal laws to protect the rights of migrant workers.

Huerta has received many awards and honors. In 1993, she became the first Hispanic American inducted into the National Women's Hall of Fame. In 1998, she received the Eleanor Roosevelt Award for Human Rights from Presi-dent Bill Clinton. And in 2012, she received the Presidential Medal of Freedom from President Barack Obama.

percent of Hispanic men and 25 percent of Hispanic women had earned a bachelor's degree or higher, compared to 41 percent of white men and 48 percent of white women. This means that some of the highest-paying jobs in the modern economy are not open to them.

Some of the differences in educational attainment can be at-tributed to the places where many Hispanic Americans grew up and the places where they live today—which historically have also been shaped by discrimination.

Housing Discrimination

The Fair Housing Act of 1968 made illegal the banking practice of routinely denying mortgages to minorities who lived in poor neighborhoods—a practice known as redlining. The legislation also prevents intentionally segregated housing, making it illegal for landlords to refuse to rent or sell homes to people just because they are a certain race or ethnicity. The effect of discriminatory housing and lending policies continues to have a powerful impact on Hispanic families nonetheless.

Decades of housing discrimination and unfair lending practices prior to 1968 forced most minorities into overcrowded, run-down neighborhoods. Today, 75 percent of formerly redlined neighborhoods continue to struggle economically, with most residents living at or below the poverty line, according to a study by the National Community Reinvestment Coalition (NCRC). "It's as if some of these places have been trapped in the past, locking neighborhoods into concentrated poverty,"[47] says NCRC director of research Jason Richardson. Meanwhile, the NCRC found that 91 percent of the former nicer neighborhoods are home to upper-income residents, most of whom are white.

Studies have found that residents of poor neighborhoods have less access to quality education and health care, which has a huge effect on their future employment prospects and quality of life. For example, schools in poor communities are less likely to offer advanced science classes, which can guide students into high-paying science, technology, engineering, and math (STEM) occupations. The National Science Foundation reported that while Hispanics make up 16 percent of the US workforce, they account for only about 6 percent of scientists and engineers. Hispanic students also drop out of STEM programs at a much higher rate than white students. Living in a poor neighborhood can even affect a person's brain—a recent study found that the intelligence quotient (IQ) of those who lived in economically disadvantaged areas was four to eight points lower than the IQ of those who lived in middle-class or upper-class neighborhoods.

The Wealth Gap

Historically, redlining and discrimination prevented Hispanic American families from accumulating wealth, a key step needed to escape from poor neighborhoods. Home ownership is one of the fastest ways to build wealth, but Hispanic Americans remain far behind whites in this regard. A 2019 study found that 54 percent of Hispanic families rent their homes, compared to just 28 percent of white families. Hispanics also tend to pay higher rents in proportion to their wages—57 percent of Hispanic families are considered "burdened" because they spend more than 30 percent of their monthly income on housing. In addition, white families are more than five times as likely to inherit valuable assets from their parents or grandparents, which increases their overall wealth. Consequently, there is a wide wealth gap. According to recent data from the Federal Reserve, the average white American family has assets worth $171,000; the average Hispanic family's assets are worth just $21,000.

Unfortunately, the laws have not completely erased discriminatory practices. A recent study by the US Department of Housing and Urban Development (HUD) involved sending pairs of people—one white and one a person of color—to inquire separately about buying or renting a home or apartment. "In one rental test, the white tester arrived first and asked to see a two-bedroom apartment," recounted the HUD report. "The agent showed him the available two-bedroom unit as well as a one-bedroom apartment and provided application information for both units. The Hispanic tester arrived two hours later at the same office, but was told that nothing was available."[48] This sort of discrimination increases the cost of housing for Hispanics while simultaneously restricting their options. Overall, the HUD study found that Hispanics seeking to buy a house are told about 12.5 percent fewer properties than whites are and are shown 7.5 percent fewer homes. Hispanic renters are more likely than equally qualified whites to be told that no apartments are available.

Compounding the problem is that many Hispanics, particularly recent immigrants, do not understand their rights under the fair housing laws or are confused by the system due to the language barrier. "While the terms 'Latino' and 'immigrant' may not be synonymous, both groups experience housing discrimination in startlingly similar ways," concludes Juliana Gonzalez-Crussi, a member of Chicago's advisory council on housing equity. "Both Latinos and immigrants grapple with a fear of retaliation for filing complaints, challenges related to language differences, and a cultural unfamiliarity that may include a fear of institutions and distrust of government."[49]

> "Both Latinos and immigrants grapple with a fear of retaliation for filing complaints, challenges related to language differences, and a cultural unfamiliarity that may include a fear of institutions and distrust of government."[49]
>
> —Juliana Gonzalez-Crussi, member of Chicago's advisory council on housing equity

An Underlying Cause of Discrimination

In recent years, many Americans have gained a greater understanding of the concept of "implicit bias"—the subconscious attitudes or stereotypes that affect a person's interactions with someone of a different race, religion, or other group. Numerous scientific studies have confirmed that nearly everyone has these unconscious biases.

Implicit biases are formed over a lifetime and do not necessarily align with a person's conscious beliefs; for example, many Americans condemn attacks like the El Paso shooting or the hateful rhetoric of white supremacist or anti-immigrant groups. Many whites admire Hispanics who have fought against racial prejudice, such as baseball star Roberto Clemente and labor and equality activists Dolores Huerta and César Chávez. And since 2016, many Americans of all colors and backgrounds have spoken out strongly against Trump's more controversial immigration policies. Even well-intentioned white people, however, may unconsciously hold negative beliefs about Hispanics due to racial stereotypes. These biases are reflected in discriminatory employment and housing practices as well as in the ways that Hispanics are treated daily by police officers, teachers, business owners, and others.

President Barack Obama presents civil rights leader Dolores Huerta with the Presidential Medal of Freedom in 2012. Even people who admire someone like Huerta might harbor unconscious biases.

Dealing with bias fueled unconsciously by stereotypes is "something that everybody has to grapple with," notes Jennifer Eberhardt, a Stanford University professor who studies implicit bias. "We're living in a society where we're absorbing images and ideas all the time and it takes over who we are and how we see the world."[50]

In one recent study, Eberhardt analyzed twenty-eight thousand police stops that occurred in California during 2013 and 2014. She and her team found that officers handcuffed 25 percent of minorities who were detained, even when no arrest was made. Only 7 percent of whites were handcuffed. Another study, conducted in 2012 at the University of Colorado, examined how police officers responded when asked to immediately react in a "shoot/don't shoot" situation involving people of different races. The study found that officers were more likely to shoot black or Hispanic suspects than white or Asian ones. "The degree of bias shown by police officers . . . was related to contact, attitudes, and stereotypes," concluded the study's authors, adding that "overestimation of community violent crime correlated with greater bias toward Latinos."[51]

The problem of implicit bias extends into other areas as well, including health care. A 2018 study found that Hispanic men in California are 21 percent less likely to receive the best treatment for high-risk prostate cancer than are white men. Even after screening for other factors, such as a patient's ability to pay or whether the ideal treatment was available at medical clinics in the patient's county, the study's authors concluded that implicit bias accounted for the disparity. "Implicit bias is pervasive in our society, and addressing it at a societal level is a complex task," explains Daphne Lichtensztajn, an epidemiologist at the University of California, San Francisco; "however, acknowledging its existence and increasing awareness is a crucial first step. As individuals become more mindful of their spontaneous reactions to people, they can begin to check these unconscious responses and make conscious efforts to change them."[52]

> "Implicit bias is pervasive in our society, and addressing it at a societal level is a complex task."[52]
>
> —Daphne Lichtensztajn, epidemiologist

Challenging Implicit Biases

Becoming aware of implicit biases and taking time to think through decisions can help people reduce discriminatory behavior. Eberhardt says, "There are certain conditions under which we become more vulnerable to it: when we're thinking fast and moving fast. We can slow down and make a shift so we're less likely to act on bias."[53]

To address workplace discrimination, some businesses have slowed their hiring process, implementing new procedures meant to remove bias toward minority applicants. An approach that is

53

Hispanics and Redlining

During the Great Depression of the 1930s, the Federal Housing Administration (FHA) was created to underwrite mortgage loans made by banks and private lenders so that Americans could purchase their own homes. The FHA promised to insure banks for their non-risky investments, even if the homeowner proved unable to pay back the loan.

To identify low-risk investments, the FHA produced detailed maps of American cities and towns. The nicest neighborhoods, where mostly white people lived, were marked green or blue on the FHA maps. They were considered the safest investments. Integrated neighborhoods, where both white and nonwhite families lived, were riskier investments and were marked yellow. Neighborhoods where the population was predominantly black or Hispanic were marked red on the maps. These areas were not eligible for FHA-insured mortgages.

Realtors and homeowners usually refused to sell homes in the green or blue neighborhoods to minorities, because such integration would lower property values and could shift a neighborhood into the "yellow" category. Banks were very selective in the loans they made in the yellow neighborhoods, and minorities rarely qualified. And the banks almost always refused to make loans in the red areas because those loans were considered too risky and so were not insured in case of default. The practice of denying loans based on the racial characteristic of a neighborhood became known as redlining.

Between 1934 and 1962, the FHA and other federal government agencies financed more than $120 billion worth of new housing. Just 2 percent of that went to Hispanic or black families that wanted to purchase a home.

becoming popular, called "blind recruitment," involves eliminating information that could be used to categorize candidates—such as their name, gender, or age—from their résumé before hiring managers review it. Names are removed because studies have shown that people with ethnic names are 50 percent less likely to get a job interview than those with names that sounded or looked more "white."

Other businesses have tried to train employees to recognize their implicit biases. In May 2018, the coffee chain Starbucks closed more than eight thousand of its stores for a day so that nearly 17,500 employees could take part in a training session to learn more about unconscious racial bias. Other companies, such as Google, the consulting firm Deloitte, and restaurant chains like Buffalo Wild Wings and Papa John's, have followed suit. "These . . . courses are intended to foster diversity and inclusion by making employees more aware of unconsciously believed negative stereotypes," explains Tomas Chamorro-Premuzic, an executive at an employment firm. "The idea is that if we can combat our underlying biases, we'll decrease discriminatory behaviors at work and level the playing field for women and underrepresented minorities."[54]

Ultimately, the best way to reduce or eliminate discrimination in the workplace, in housing, or elsewhere in society is through education. School curricula should include information about the contribution of women, immigrants, and Hispanic Americans and other minorities. The media can combat stereotypes by presenting Hispanic culture in a positive light. The good news is that these efforts are already being made in much of the United States today.

CHAPTER FIVE

Here to Stay

One of the highlights of the Super Bowl LIV halftime show on February 4, 2020, came toward the end of the performance, as eleven-year-old Emme Maribel Muñiz sang a chorus of "Born in the U.S.A." while her mother, superstar Puerto Rican American Jennifer "J. Lo" Lopez, belted out the lyrics to her Latin pop anthem "Let's Get Loud." Their joyous back-and-forth duet sent a clear message to the more than 100 million people who were watching: Hispanic Americans are not going anywhere.

The entire fourteen-minute-long halftime show was a celebration of Latin culture and its place in America. Along with J. Lo, the show featured Colombian pop star Shakira, reggaeton singer J Balvin, and Puerto Rican rapper Bad Bunny, along with a host of dancers and musicians. The performers sang upbeat songs in both Spanish and English and danced vigorously in a variety of popular Afro-Caribbean styles: reggaeton, salsa, champeta, and mapalé. At one point, Lopez sported a feathered cape that featured the Puerto Rican flag on one side and the American flag on the other. This was one of many acknowledgments of her heritage—Lopez was born in the New York City borough the Bronx, but her parents are American citizens from Puerto Rico. Her energetic display made many of Puerto Rico's residents proud. "It's a validity that we are here," says William Ramírez-Hernández, executive director of the ACLU of Puerto Rico, who watched the show from the Puerto Rican capital city of San Juan. "We are people to be respected."[55]

Afterward, most Americans gushed about the show. *USA Today* called it "one of the best, most empowering and flat-out fun Super Bowl halftimes of the past decade."[56] Hispanic Americans appreciated the tributes to their cultures as well as the underlying political statement about their place in the United States. "At a time when the [Hispanic] community has felt under attack, whether from visceral rhetoric, horribly restrictive policies, or literal acts of violence, it felt deeply assuring to see two iconic Latinas leave their mark on the most overtly American sporting event," notes journalist

The 2020 Super Bowl halftime show was a celebration of Latin culture and its place in America. Superstar Jennifer Lopez (pictured performing in Brazil) was one of the featured performers.

Edwin Rios. "It felt more of an embrace of Latinx culture than an embrace of overt patriotism seen in previous halftime shows."[57]

Changing Attitudes

The Super Bowl halftime show reflected the ways that Latin music and culture have become firmly entrenched in American life. Latin music is one of the most popular genres in the United States today and in 2019 surpassed the country music genre in album sales.

Although bias and discrimination clearly remain problems, in certain important respects there has never been a better time to be Hispanic in America. More Hispanics are finding gainful employment in the United States than ever before. An October 2019 report by the US Department of Labor found that the jobless rate for Hispanics had reached a record low of 3.9 percent. Additionally, the percentage of Hispanic families living in poverty has fallen steadily over the past few years. Data from the US Census Bureau's 2019 report *Income and Poverty in the United States* indicate that the poverty rate among Hispanic Americans declined sharply from 2015 to 2017 (the most recent data available). As of early 2020, 18.1 percent of Hispanic Americans lived in poverty, the lowest rate since the government began tracking this information in the early 1970s.

And for many Hispanic families, the best days could be ahead. Economists have found that second-generation Hispanic Americans do much better than their parents economically and socially. They are getting better educations and are more likely to move into the middle or upper socioeconomic classes. "The new evidence tells a mostly optimistic story," writes Van C. Tran, a Columbia University sociologist who studies immigrant assimilation. "The Latino second generation will most likely

"The Latino second generation will most likely follow the time-honored path of European immigrants and their descendants, who achieved parity with the White American mainstream over the course of three generations."[58]

—Van C. Tran, Columbia University sociology professor

Hispanics in the News Media

Hispanic news reporters and editors, who could push for stories that reflect the Hispanic community and its important issues, might do a lot to counter negative stereotypes. The American Society of News Editors (ASNE) has been encouraging increased newsroom diversity since the late 1970s; however, ASNE's most recent diversity survey found that approximately 80 percent of newsroom employees are white. Although Hispanics make up 18 percent of the population, they hold less than 7 percent of newsroom jobs.

Even in the places where Hispanics are most populous, they are rarely represented in newsroom staffs. Less than 5 percent of the political reporters for the *New York Times*, *Washington Post*, and *USA Today* are Hispanic. Southern California's largest public radio station, KPCC, has just one Hispanic radio show host; across the nation, only 6 percent of National Public Radio employees are Hispanic. Only 15 percent of the *Los Angeles Times*'s newsroom staff is Hispanic, even though Hispanics make up 50 percent of the population of Los Angeles County.

Esmeralda Bermudez, a *Los Angeles Times* reporter, feels that being the daughter of immigrants from Mexico makes her well suited to write on issues that affect Hispanic Americans, such as the impact of Trump's family separation policy at the border. "I have felt child separation on my skin," Bermudez explains. "There is a connection that I am able to make that someone who basically has never gone through that would never even think about."

Quoted in Diego Pineda, "Surveys on Newsroom Diversity Conclude That the Numbers Are Not Changing," *Latino Reporter*, July 19, 2018. http://latinoreporter.org.

---

follow the time-honored path of European immigrants and their descendants, who achieved parity with the White American mainstream over the course of three generations. . . . The barriers confronting Latinos are significant, but not insurmountable."[58]

Finally, the traditional view of the American "melting pot," in which immigrants abandoned their Old World cultures and were completely assimilated into American society, is changing. Many people today prefer the metaphor of the "salad bowl," in which separate ingredients work together yet retain some of their original characteristics. And as Americans gain a greater awareness of implicit bias and its effect on discrimination, they are more likely to reject arguments of anti-immigrant groups that Hispanics have trouble fitting in to the United States. "Those who tell Latinos to assimilate often fail to acknowledge the centuries of exclusion, racism and systemic discrimination that have slowed Latinos' economic and social mobility," writes Suzanne Gamboa. "Racism puts up practical roadblocks to integration and participation, preventing Latinos from being accepted as 'assimilated.'"[59]

Making Their Voices Heard

One way that Hispanics are fighting to preserve their rights is through greater participation in elections. The 2020 presidential election marked the first time that Hispanics made up the largest racial or ethnic minority in the voting public. The Pew Research Center estimated that 32 million Hispanics were eligible to vote in 2020—more than 13 percent of the total electorate.

The number of Hispanic voters should continue to grow rapidly over the next few decades. As of 2020, only about half of the approximately 60 million Hispanics who live in the United States were eligible to vote. This is mainly because the Hispanic population is much younger, on average, than other American racial or ethnic groups, with 18.6 million Hispanics having not yet reached the voting age of eighteen as of 2020. Another 11.3 million Hispanics are immigrants who have not yet achieved citizenship; some will eventually be naturalized, making them eligible to participate in US elections.

As the number of Hispanic voters grows, so will their political clout. Until recently, Hispanics were among the least likely Americans to vote in state or federal elections. But since 2014 several organizations have launched voter-registration drives, seeking to increase Hispanic participation in the political process. The Latino Vote Project, which tracked voter turnout in the 2014, 2016, and

2018 election cycles, found that 40 percent of eligible Hispanic voters went to the polls in 2018, a record high. The number of Hispanic voters nationwide increased from 6.8 million in 2014 to 11.7 million by 2018 and was expected to exceed 13 million by 2021.

These voter registration and education efforts are needed to close the gap in representation. A 2018 study by the National Association of Latino Elected and Appointed Officials found that, nationwide, only about sixty-seven hundred Hispanics held local, state, and federal elected offices. That works out to a rate of Hispanic representation of around 1.2 percent. Although Hispanics are the largest ethnic group in California, at 40 percent of the population, they hold just 24 percent of the seats in the state legislature. The 116th US Congress, elected in 2018, has been called "the most representative of Latinos in history,"[60] yet Hispanics held just 38 of the 435 seats in the House of Representatives and 4 of 100 seats in the Senate.

Actresses (from left) Zoe Saldana, Eva Longoria, Gina Rodriguez, America Ferrera, and Rosario Dawson host a rally to encourage Florida's Latino voters to go to the polls in the 2018 midterm elections.

"Every bill matters," points out Matt Barreto, a UCLA professor of political science and Chicano studies. "There's a Latino angle to education reform, economic policies, health care. These aren't white issues; these are everyone's issues. Black, Latino, Asian communities: we should all be equally represented. That's what we should expect in a healthy democracy."[61]

Overall, though, the signs here are positive as well. Voter registration programs are clearly having an effect, and hard-line immigration policies have motivated many people to vote for candidates who favor a more moderate approach. The number of Hispanics serving in Congress has nearly doubled since 2006, and more Hispanics than ever are serving in high-profile state or national political offices. All of them have their own immigrant histories to share.

Suzanna Martinez's grandparents came to the United States from Mexico in the early twentieth century; in 2011, she took office as governor of New Mexico, becoming the first Hispanic woman to be elected a state governor. The Republican served in that position until 2019. In 2009, Sonia Sotomayor was the first Hispanic woman appointed to the US Supreme Court; the Bronx native's parents had emigrated from Puerto Rico during World War II. Former San Antonio mayor Julián Castro served in the Obama administration and was a candidate for the Democratic Party's presidential nomination in 2020; his grandmother came from Mexico to San Antonio in 1922 when she was eight years old. Perhaps the most notable is New York representative Alexandria Ocasio-Cortez, a Bronx native of Puerto Rican descent who was elected in 2018. She has become a powerful voice in Congress for the progressive wing of the Democratic Party.

Going Beyond Stereotypes

Many Hispanics have begun to push back against negative stereotypes that others have used to define them. These include the images of young Hispanics as drug smugglers, gang members,

or illiterate school dropouts; of Hispanic women as promiscuous; of Hispanic men as aggressive and macho; and of Hispanic immigrants as being in the country illegally, taking jobs away from American workers.

Unfortunately, these negative stereotypes are reinforced by the ways that Hispanics are often portrayed in the news or entertainment media. In a study conducted for the National Hispanic Media Coalition, non-Hispanic participants were asked about the sort of roles that Hispanic film and television actors play. The findings were telling: 71 percent said they saw Latinos in criminal or gang member roles "very often" or "sometimes," and over 60 percent regularly saw Hispanics in the role of gardeners, landscapers, housekeepers, or maids. On the other hand, only 5 percent saw Hispanics in roles as teachers, nurses/doctors, or lawyers/judges. "Negative portrayals of Latinos and immigrants are pervasive in news and

Finding a Voice Through Poetry

In 2015, the Library of Congress chose award-winning Mexican American poet Juan Felipe Herrera as the twenty-first US poet laureate, the nation's "official" poet. The first Hispanic US poet laureate, Herrera created a website called La Casa de Colores ("The House of Colors"). In a section titled "La Familia," Herrera invites Americans of all races and backgrounds to contribute verses to what he described as "an epic poem of all our voices and styles and experiences."

In an interview with *Gulf Stream Magazine*, Herrera explains the purpose that he envisions for "La Familia":

> Because of the tidal wave of media technology, new scenes, new stories come in every day, but the scenes and stories of working class people don't always make it to prime time. So the idea is to bring in those voices, open up the media gates through the Library of Congress website to give them national and global exposure. And then to see it, to have our bilingual students or our bilingual families in our communities, saying, "I can't believe it. This is my poem about my migrant experience. There it is!"

The experiences of Hispanic migrant workers and immigrants as well as the problems of indigenous communities are essential themes of Herrera's poetry. He was born in 1948 to migrant farmworkers and grew up living in tents and shacks in the farming communities of California's San Joaquin Valley. "La Familia" can be read at the Library of Congress's website.

Quoted in Ariel Francisco, "Interview with Juan Felipe Herrera, 2015," *Gulf Stream Magazine*, no. 14, 2015. https://gulfstreamlitmag.com.

entertainment media," concludes the study. "Consequently, non-Latinos commonly believe many negative stereotypes about these groups are true."[62]

The news media can play an important role in eliminating stereotypes. In recent years, some media outlets have begun airing more positive stories about Hispanics and their experiences in the United States; for example, in 2020 the newspaper *USA Today* launched a series called Hecho en USA ("Made in America") to provide broader coverage of Hispanic issues. "Media coverage of Hispanics tends to focus on immigration and crime, instead of how Latino families live, work and learn in their hometowns," noted the newspaper. "Hecho en USA tells the stories of the nation's 59.9 million Latinos—a growing economic and cultural force, many of whom are increasingly born in the United States."[63]

"The news media industry must play a role, and that role starts with reviewing the way it portrays Latinos in its coverage," agrees Graciela Mochkofsky, adding,

> The wonderful complexity of Latino communities has for too long been lost on mainstream America, as Latinos have been misunderstood, underreported, stigmatized, and grouped into an indistinguishable mass only defined by the immigrant experience and by assumed fluency in Spanish, which many, but not all, Latinos actually speak. In fact, Latinos in the United States comprise a wildly diverse population.[64]

What the Future Holds

At a 2017 conference at Yale Law School, law professor Gerald Torres described being confronted by an anti-immigrant nativist, who told him that he did not belong and should go back where he came from. Torres, who is of Spanish and Native American heritage, delivered a simple yet effective response. "One side of my family has been here since 1620," he said, "and the other side for 12,000 years."[65]

As Torres implied, Hispanic Americans have deep roots in North America, and they are not going anywhere. Of the nearly 60 million Hispanics who live in the United States today, roughly 79 percent are US citizens, and 67 percent were born in America.

About 78 percent have lived in the United States for at least ten years, and 46 percent for more than twenty-one years.

Rather than being forcibly assimilated into American culture, this growing Hispanic community will have an opportunity to transform the culture over the next forty years. The US Census Bureau projects that the Hispanic American population will grow to more than 111 million by the year 2060 and will represent more than a quarter of the total US population. Much of that growth will come from the children and grandchildren of Hispanics who are already living here, sharing experiences with Americans of other races and ethnicities.

Mochkofsky sums up the issue this way: "Latinos should be seen for what we are: not 'the other,' but a part of 'us.' We're given broad labels like 'Latino' or 'Hispanic.' If we were considered part of *us*, part of America, then there wouldn't be a need to define us with any other name."[66]

SOURCE NOTES

Introduction: Murders in El Paso

1. Quoted in Yasmeen Abutaleb, "What's Inside the Hate-Filled Manifesto Linked to the Alleged El Paso Shooter," *Washington Post*, August 4, 2019. www.washingtonpost.com.
2. Quoted in Lauren Villagran, "El Paso Shooting Suspect's Hate-Filled Writing Used Similar Language as Trump Campaign," *El Paso Times*, August 6, 2019. www.elpasotimes.com.
3. Quoted in Adeel Hassan, "Hate-Crime Violence Hits 16-Year High, F.B.I. Reports," *New York Times*, November 12, 2019. www.nytimes.com.
4. Camilo M. Ortiz, "Latinos Nowhere in Sight: Erased by Racism, Nativism, the Black-White Binary, and Authoritarianism," *Rutgers Race & the Law Review*, vol. 29, 2012. www.racism.org.

Chapter One: A History of Second-Class Citizenship

5. Digital History, "Treaty of Guadalupe Hidalgo (1848), article IX." www.digitalhistory.uh.edu.
6. Linda Heidenreich, "Greaser Act (1855)," in *Latino History and Culture: An Encyclopedia*, edited by David J. Leonard and Carmen R. Lugo-Lugo. New York: Sharpe, 2010, p. 218.
7. William D. Carrigan and Clive Webb, *Forgotten Dead: Mob Violence Against Mexicans in the United States, 1848–1928*. New York: Oxford University Press, 2013, p. 2.
8. José Luis Morín, ed., *Latinos and Criminal Justice: A History*. Santa Barbara, CA: Greenwood, 2016, p. 15.
9. Ortiz, "Latinos Nowhere in Sight."
10. Quoted in Terry Gross, "America's Forgotten History of Mexican-American 'Repatriation,'" *Fresh Air*, National Public Radio, September 10, 2015. https://www.npr.org.

11. Erin Blakemore, "The Largest Mass Deportation in American History," History Channel website, March 23, 2018; updated June 18, 2019. https://history.com.

12. Charles Hirschman, "The Impact of Immigration on American Society," *Eurozine*, May 11, 2007. www.eurozine.com.

Chapter Two: Inciting Violence

13. Quoted in John Ismay, "Suspect Charged with Hate Crime in Acid Attack on Hispanic Man," *New York Times*, November 7, 2019. www.nytimes.com.

14. Quoted in Karma Allen, "Milwaukee Man Charged with Hate Crime in Racist Acid Attack, Authorities Say," ABC News, November 6, 2019. https://abcnews.go.com.

15. Quoted in Nicole Wiesenthal, "Man Beaten, Frat House Defaced in Politics-Laced Crimes," *Gainesville (FL) Sun*, November 22, 2016. www.gainesville.com.

16. Quoted in CBS News, "Officers Fired, Charged After Allegedly Beating Man and Calling Him "Fake American," July 26, 2018. www.cbsnews.com.

17. Quoted in Lorraine Boissoneault, "How the 19th-Century Know Nothing Party Reshaped American Politics," *Smithsonian Magazine*, January 26, 2017. www.smithsonianmag.com.

18. Immigration Restriction League, "Publication No. 38: Immigration Figures for 1903," Gilder Lehrman Institute of American History. www.gilderlehrman.org.

19. Quoted in Amy R. Connolly, "Pro-Trump Robocall: 'Don't Vote for a Cuban,'" United Press International, February 25, 2016. www.upi.com.

20. Donald Trump, "Interview with Don Lemon," CNN, December 9, 2015. www.cnn.com.

21. Quoted in Domenico Montanaro, "Democratic Candidates Call Trump a White Supremacist, a Label Some Say Is 'Too Simple,'" National Public Radio, August 15, 2019. www.npr.org.

22. Quoted in Lorenzo Ferrigno, "Donald Trump: Boston Beating Is 'Terrible,'" CNN, August 21, 2015. www.cnn.com.

23. Quoted in Ferrigno, "Donald Trump."

24. Quoted in Matthew Choi, "Trump: Military Will Defend Border from Caravan 'Invasion,'" Politico, October 29, 2018. www.politico.com.

25. Quoted in Suzanne Gamboa, "Anti-Hispanic Violence That Pierced El Paso Has Been Part of Texas' History," NBC News, August 16, 2019. www.nbcnews.com.

26. Quoted in Dani Anguiano, "'It's Worse than Ever': How Latinos Are Changing Their Lives in Trump's America," *The Guardian* (Manchester, UK), October 7, 2019. www.theguardian.com.

27. Graciela Mochkofsky, "The Vital Importance of Learning to See Latinos in Trump's America," *New Yorker*, August 10, 2019. www.newyorker.com.

28. Mochkofsky, "The Vital Importance of Learning to See Latinos in Trump's America."

29. Quoted in Rafael Bernal, "Hispanics Say Trump's Words Are Too Little, Too Late," *The Hill* (Washington, DC), August 7, 2019. https://thehill.com.

30. Quoted in Rishika Dugyala, "El Paso Congresswoman to Trump: Don't Come Here," Politico, August 5, 2019. www.politico.com.

31. Quoted in Anguiano, "'It's Worse than Ever.'"

Chapter Three: The Language of America

32. Quoted in Bill Chappell, "Americans Who Were Detained After Speaking Spanish in Montana Sue US Border Agency," National Public Radio, February 15, 2019. www.npr.org.

33. Quoted in Roberto Rey Agudo, "This Is America: Speak Whatever Language You Want," *The Hill* (Washington, DC), February 25, 2019. https://thehill.com.

34. Quoted in KRTV-3 (Great Falls, MT), "Judge Hears Case Involving Border Patrol Questioning of 2 Women in Havre," October 3, 2019. www.krtv.com.

35. Quoted in Matt Volz, "Women Leave Havre over Border Agency Lawsuit Backlash," Montana Public Radio, September 20, 2019. www.mtpr.org.

36. Quoted in Anguiano, "'It's Worse than Ever.'"

37. Quoted in Ludmila Leiva, "Eight Latinx Professionals Open Up About Discrimination in the Workplace," Refinery29, October 8, 2018. www.refinery29.com.

38. Quoted in Beatriz Diez, "'English Only': The Movement to Limit Spanish Speaking in the US," BBC News, December 3, 2019. www.bbc.com.

39. K.C. McAlpin, "Why English Should Be the Official Language of the United States," ProEnglish. https://proenglish.org.

40. Christopher Ingraham, "Millions of US Citizens Don't Speak English to One Another. That's Not a Problem," *Washington Post*, May 21, 2018. www.washingtonpost.com.

41. Quoted in Suzanne Gamboa, "Racism, Not a Lack of Assimilation, Is the Real Problem Facing Latinos in America," NBC News, February 26, 2019. www.nbcnews.com.

42. Quoted in Ed O'Keefe, "Tim Kaine Can Speak Spanish. But Most Hispanics Don't Care," *Washington Post*, July 24, 2016. www.washingtonpost.com.

43. Nelson Flores, "Tim Kaine Speaks Spanish. Does He Want a Cookie?," *HuffPost* (blog), July 26, 2017. www.huffpos.com.

44. Steven Bender, "Consumer Protection for Latinos: Overcoming Language Fraud," *American University Law Review*, vol. 45, no. 4, 1996, p. 1095.

Chapter Four: Dealing with Discrimination

45. Lincoln Quillian et al., "Meta-Analysis of Field Experiments Shows No Change in Racial Discrimination in Hiring over Time," *Proceedings of the National Academy of Sciences*, vol. 114, October 10, 2017. www.pnas.org.

46. National Partnership for Women and Families, "Quantifying America's Gender Wage Gap by Race/Ethnicity," fact sheet, March 2020. www.nationalpartnership.org.

47. Quoted in Tracy Jan, "Redlining Was Banned 50 Years Ago. It's Still Hurting Minorities Today," *Washington Post*, March 28, 2018. www.washingtonpost.com.

48. US Department of Housing and Urban Development, "Housing Discrimination Against Racial and Ethnic Minorities 2012." www.huduser.gov.

49. Juliana Gonzalez-Crussi, "HUD: Yes, Latinos Still Experience Housing Discrimination," Latino Policy Forum, August 5, 2013. www.latinopolicyforum.org.

50. Quoted in Belinda Luscombe, "What Police Departments and the Rest of Us Can Do to Overcome Implicit Bias, According to an Expert," *Time*, March 27, 2019. https://time.com.

51. Melody S. Sadler et al., "The World Is Not Black and White: Racial Bias in the Decision to Shoot in a Multiethnic Context," *Journal of Social Issues,* vol. 68, no. 2, 2012, p. 286.

52. Quoted in PR Newswire, "Latino Men Are Much Less Likely to Receive Optimal Treatment for High Risk Prostate Can-

cer than White Men, According to New Research in *JNCCN*," November 15, 2018. www.prnewswire.com.

53. Quoted in Luscombe, "What Police Departments and the Rest of Us Can Do to Overcome Implicit Bias, According to an Expert."

54. Tomas Chamorro-Premuzic, "Implicit Bias Training Doesn't Work," Bloomberg News, January 4, 2020. www.bloomberg.com.

Chapter Five: Here to Stay

55. Quoted in Emily Codik, "Shakira and Jennifer Lopez's Super Bowl Halftime Show Wasn't 'Inappropriate.' It Was a Latin Party at Its Finest," *Washington Post*, February 4, 2020. www.washingtonpost.com.

56. Patrick Ryan, "Jennifer Lopez and Shakira Dazzle in One of the Best Super Bowl Halftime Shows in Memory," *USA Today*, February 3, 2020. www.usatoday.com.

57. Quoted in Justin Agrelo, "The Messy Racial Politics of the Super Bowl Halftime Show," *Mother Jones*, February 7, 2020. www.motherjones.com.

58. Van C. Tran, "Social Mobility Among Second-Generation Latinos," *Contexts*, Spring 2016. https://journals.sagepub.com.

59. Gamboa, "Racism, Not a Lack of Assimilation, Is the Real Problem Facing Latinos in America."

60. Dianna M. Náñez, "Latinos Make Up Only 1 Percent of All Local and Federal Elected Officials, and That's a Big Problem," *USA Today*, January 31, 2020. www.usatoday.com.

61. Quoted in Náñez, "Latinos Make Up Only 1 Percent of All Local and Federal Elected Officials, and That's a Big Problem."

62. National Hispanic Media Coalition, "The Impact of Media Stereotypes on Opinions and Attitudes Toward Latinos," September 2012. www.chicano.ucla.edu.

63. Quoted in Náñez, "Latinos Make Up Only 1 Percent of All Local and Federal Elected Officials, and That's a Big Problem."

64. Mochkofsky, "The Vital Importance of Learning to See Latinos in Trump's America."

65. Quoted in Ed Morales, "Opinion: How Do We Build the Future of Latinos in the Age of Trump?," NBC News, May 15, 2017. www.nbcnews.com.

66. Mochkofsky, "The Vital Importance of Learning to See Latinos in Trump's America."

ORGANIZATIONS AND WEBSITES

Latino Americans—www.pbs.org/latino-americans

The companion website for the PBS documentary series *Latino Americans*, which chronicles the history of Hispanics in the United States through hundreds of interviews. The programs, video links, a timeline of helpful dates, and blog posts are available in both English and Spanish.

Mexican American Legislative Leadership Foundation
http://mallfoundation.org

This nonprofit foundation works with Hispanic youth in Texas to develop a professional understanding of government while encouraging civic participation. Its website includes links to various government organizations and an application form for the Moreno/Rangel Legislative Leadership scholarship.

Pew Hispanic Center—www.pewhispanic.org

The Pew Hispanic Center is a nonpartisan research organization that seeks to improve understanding of the US Hispanic population. Its website includes research and public opinion surveys on various social, economic, and political topics involving Hispanics in the United States.

UnidosUS—www.unidosus.org

UnidosUS is the nation's largest Latino civil rights and advocacy organization. The organization was founded in 1968 as the National Council of La Raza. The website includes informative links on issues of interest, such as civil rights and criminal justice, education, health care, immigration, and voting.

Univision—www.univision.net

Univision is the largest Spanish-language media company serving the United States. Its website includes video links to news, entertainment, and sports reports, as well as information about daily programming on the network.

US Department of Labor—www.dol.gov

The US Department of Labor oversees the administration of federal labor laws that guarantee fair, safe, and healthy working conditions, including eliminating employment discrimination. The site provides information about different types of discrimination, as well as the rights of workers and the protections that they are entitled to under the law.

US Equal Employment Opportunities Commission
www.eeoc.gov

The commission's website lists the types of workplace discrimination and provides information about how workers are protected by federal laws.

FOR FURTHER RESEARCH

Books

Jessica Lavariega Conforti, ed., *Latinos in the American Political System*. Santa Barbara, CA: ABC-CLIO, 2019.

Joe R. Feagin and José A. Cobas, *Latinos Facing Racism: Discrimination, Resistance, and Endurance*. New York: Routledge, 2016.

Michael Lewis, *The Fifth Risk*. New York: Norton, 2018.

John Moore, *Undocumented: Immigration and the Militarization of the United States–Mexico Border*. New York: Powerhouse, 2018.

Nicholas Villanueva Jr., *The Lynching of Mexicans in the Texas Borderlands*. Albuquerque: University of New Mexico Press, 2017.

Internet Sources

Erin Blakemore, "The Largest Mass Deportation in American History," History Channel website, June 18, 2019. https://history.com.

Lorraine Boissoneault, "How the 19th-Century Know Nothing Party Reshaped American Politics," *Smithsonian Magazine*, January 26, 2017. www.smithsonianmag.com.

Suzanne Gamboa, "Anti-Hispanic Violence That Pierced El Paso Has Been Part of Texas' History," NBC News, August 16, 2019. www.nbcnews.com.

Adeel Hassan, "Hate-Crime Violence Hits 16-Year High, F.B.I. Reports," *New York Times*, November 12, 2019. www.nytimes.com.

Charles Hirschman, "The Impact of Immigration on American Society," *Eurozine*, May 11, 2007. www.eurozine.com.

Becky Little, "Why Mexican Americans Say 'the Border Crossed Us,'" History Channel website, October 17, 2018. www.history .com.

Graciela Mochkofsky, "The Vital Importance of Learning to See Latinos in Trump's America," *New Yorker*, August 10, 2019. www .newyorker.com.

INDEX

PICTURE CREDITS